RECEIVED
KT-520-239
30131 05806431 9
LONDON BOROUGH OF BARNET

SUPERNAN'S DAY OUT

PHIL EARLE

Illustrated by
Steve May

Barrington Stoke

First published in 2022 in Great Britain by
Barrington Stoke Ltd
18 Walker Street, Edinburgh, EH3 7LP

www.barringtonstoke.co.uk

A CIP catalogue record for this book is available from the British Library upon request

ISBN: 978-1-80090-110-0

Printed by Hussar Books, Poland

This book is in a super-readable format for young readers beginning their independent reading journey.

This book is dedicated to H.E.R.O.
(Haydn, Esther, Robyn and Oscar)

You are the fabulous 4 and
I love you very much ...

CONTENTS

CHAPTER 1

THE WORST NEWS ... EVER

Stanley is NOT a normal boy.

He may look normal: normal height, normal brown eyes, normal clothes. But don't be fooled.

Don’t be taken in by his normal-looking dog, who wees in annoying places and drives his mum mad.

Or by his dad, who looks like he works in a dull office, pushing pieces of paper around his desk so his boss doesn’t shout at him.

You see, Stanley and his dad have a secret. A wonderful secret. A secret so secret that it needs to be kept in a secret chamber at the centre of the earth, secretly guarded by a dozen fire-breathing dragons who are also really good at keeping secrets.

You see, this father and son are … superheroes.

And not just any superheroes.

They are Dynamo Dan and Super Stan. The most dynamic duo of caped crusaders to ever walk (or fly) the earth.

"Help! The world has been invaded by alien slugs from the planet Wobblebum!"

No problem. Dan and Stan will zap them in a second.

"ARGHHH! An evil crime lord has stolen every bar of chocolate on the planet!"

Don't sweat it. Dan and Stan will arrest them in a jiffy.

"Oh my lord! My toilet is blocked and it smells worse than anything I've ever smelled in my life!"

Well ... you should probably call a plumber. *Some* jobs aren't fit for superheroes as wonderful as this pair.

THAT'S how amazing they are at being superheroes. They are the best.

*

But sometimes even superheroes get tired. Sometimes they need a rest. And this was one of those times.

In the past week, Dad and Stan had stopped 27 invading UFOs, 91 kidnaps and 603 bank robberies, so you could understand why Mum was getting more than a little bit cross with them.

"You two look like you've been dragged through a hedge backwards!" she said. "Stanley, you fell asleep in your soup last night, and as for you ..." She turned to Dad with a very big frown. "You're as grumpy as a snail who's been forced to run across a desert!

“Both of you are taking the day off. No ifs, no buts. Dan, you’re going to a health spa to rest, and as for you, Stanley ...”

Stanley waited to find out what was in store for him.

“You’re not going to use your powers once today, because you’re going to spend the day with your nan.”

Stanley’s heart sank. He wanted to cry but knew his super-tears would flood the kitchen in seconds.

This was the worst news ... EVER.

CHAPTER 2
CABBAGE HOUSE

Stanley grumbled and moaned as he walked to his nan's. "Grumble ... moan ... moan ... grumble," he moaned. And grumbled.

Nan lived in an old people's home called Claridge House. *Cabbage* House, Stanley called it, as no matter what they were having for dinner there, it always smelled of cabbage. Cabbage that had been boiled for seven years in stinking puddle water.

Stanley loved his nan, of course he did. She was his dad's mum after all. But while his dad was Dynamo Dan ... well, his nan was ... different.

She was always talking about the good old days (whatever they were), her favourite thing was a weird, dull game called bingo, and worst of all she never ever called Stanley by his name. She called him *Sam*, or *Simon* and sometimes *Sharon*.

He didn't want to think about the wet, slobbery kiss she'd give him when he got there, and the click-clack of her false teeth that didn't properly fit in her mouth.

"Why did Mum give me such a boring day off?" he moaned. "At least Dad can swim or go to a gym. I have to sit and play board games ... more like *bored* games."

It was a rubbish joke, and it did not cheer Stanley up.

But when he arrived, things were not as he expected. Outside the home was a shabby old coach with a lot of old faces peering out of the dirty windows.

And waiting on the steps, leaning on a pair of walking sticks, was Nan.

"Steven!!!" she yelled. Her teeth nearly fell out of her mouth. "We've been waiting for you. We're off to the seaside!"

TWILIGHT TOURS

Stanley groaned. He could run faster than such an old bus, and he knew it would smell of cabbage. And while he loved the seaside, how was it fun to spend the day with OLD people?

It was going to be AWFUL.

CHAPTER 3
PLANE PANIC

The beach was only thirty minutes away, but it felt like they were travelling as far as Australia.

None of the windows on the coach would open, so with the summer heat and the cabbage whiff, Stanley was soon feeling very sick.

“Are we nearly there yet?” he asked his nan.

“Soon, Shaun, soon,” she replied.

“Ooooh, young people are always in a hurry these days,” said Nan’s friend Gladys. “Here, have a sweetie.” And she pushed something into Stanley’s mouth.

At last, Stanley thought, *something good to come out of the day*. But ten seconds later, he realised the sweet tasted of one thing only. You guessed it ... cabbage.

"Oooh, look at his lovely face," Gladys cooed. "That's cheered him up."

Stanley knew then that Gladys's eyesight was not that good, as his mouth and eyes were screwed up tight. The sweet was disgusting! He looked for somewhere to spit it out, but everyone was looking at him and he didn't want to seem rude or ungrateful.

“Mmmmmm,” he said. Maybe if he sucked extra hard, the sweet would be gone extra quick.

Stanley rested his face on the coach window to look outside and tried to think of something else.

The first thing he saw was a plane hurtling through the sky. But this plane wasn't on its way to a tropical island holiday. This plane's engine was making a terrible noise as if it was broken. Unless someone did something quick, then the plane was going to crash into the sea!

TOURS

CHAPTER 4
SUPERHERO MYSTERY

Stanley wanted to help. He KNEW he could help. He was Super Stan after all, but at the same time, what could he do? He was stuck on a coach and if he snuck away to change, his nan would guess about his secret superpowers.

As he tried to work out what to do, he saw something brilliant.

From out of nowhere, something bolted across the sky at the speed of light.

What is it? thought Stanley. *A missile? A super-charged flying emu?*

It was moving too quickly for Stanley to work out who or what it was.

Then something even better happened. The blur caught up with the plane.

And that's when Stanley KNEW it had to be another superhero.

But who could it be? It couldn't be Dad, as Mum had hidden his costume before he left for the spa. And if it wasn't Dad, who was it?

Stanley looked again as the plane stopped falling towards the sea. Instead, the blur helped the plane come slowly down to earth and land with a gentle bump in a farmer's field.

It was one of the greatest and bravest superhero saves ever. Stanley was excited. He wanted to know who the hero was, but he STILL had no idea.

"Wow, Nan, did you see that?" he said, turning round to ask her. But Nan was nowhere to be seen. Her seat was empty apart from a single bent knitting needle.

“Nan?” said Stanley. “Nan?” He looked everywhere for her – under the seat, even in the bag rack above the seats. But she had vanished.

“How weird,” he said, and then at last he saw her. She was pulling on her

cardigan as she hobbled from the toilet at the back of the coach.

"Sorry about that, Spencer love. I had soup for supper last night and it's playing havoc with my tummy."

Yuk! Stanley did not want to know what had happened in that toilet, or why his nan had to take her cardigan off.

There was no point talking to Nan about what he'd just seen. She was never going to believe a story about a superhero and a falling plane. She didn't even believe his name was Stanley.

But Stanley needed to work out who the superhero was, because what he had just seen was AMAZING.

CHAPTER 5
BINGO BUST

By the time they arrived at the seaside, Stanley had other things to worry about.

Some of Nan's friends wanted to ride on the donkeys, others were asking for candyfloss and sticks of rock, but Nan and Gladys only wanted one thing. A game of bingo.

There were moans and groans from the others (and Stanley), but within minutes, and after some evil looks from Nan, everyone walked (very slowly) to the bingo hall.

BINGO
KISS ME QUICK
FUN

Inside the hall, Stanley was bored silly. Bingo was just a man with a very loud voice shouting random numbers and crazy words:

"Clickety click – 66!"

"Droopy drawers – 44!"

"Doctors orders – number 9!"

Stanley wished he was somewhere else. But Nan's friends loved it, as did Nan. She went on knitting the whole time as well as marking off numbers on the card in front of her.

On it went for what felt like weeks, and Stanley almost dropped off to sleep, when ...

“STOP! THIEF!!” came the cry. Stanley jumped and sat up. There was a man in a clown mask running across the bingo-hall floor, carrying a large, bulging sack.

Suddenly Stanley felt alive. This was a crime he could foil in a heartbeat, but there wasn’t time to vanish and come back in his superhero clothes. The robber was making for the door, and when Stanley saw the size of his sack, he knew the robber was going to be a very rich man!

KISS
88
2

But just as the man was about to escape, Stanley heard a whooshing noise cut through the air, not once but twice.

Stanley had superhero vision, but he couldn't work out what was making the noise or where it had come from. All he knew was that when he turned to see what was happening, the robber was now pinned to the wall by what looked like two mini javelins.

"Whoooooa!" said Stanley, for as he looked closer he could see that the spikes hadn't hurt the man in any way. They had passed through his clothes instead and trapped him. The police burst through the door seconds later to make the arrest.

Stanley looked around. The only person who could throw with that sort of accuracy was another superhero. It took one to know one. But no matter where he looked, he couldn't see anyone who fitted the bill. Instead, all he could see was Nan, who had a big grin on her face.

"Look!" she yelled as if Stanley was deaf. "I finished knitting your jumper, Scotty!"

Stanley wanted to shout at her. First, his name was Stanley, not Scotty. And second, he wasn't ever going to wear that jumper – it was enormous!!!

He was so puzzled. He knew there was a superhero somewhere nearby. But could Stanley work out who it was? He could not.

CHAPTER 6
FIRE! FIRE!

Back outside after bingo, Stanley was in a bad mood now. Not because of hanging out with his nan and her friends.

Well, that didn't help, but what really made him cross was not being able to work out who kept saving the day. Especially as HE wanted in on the action too.

He thought about asking Nan, then changed his mind. Then he decided he HAD to ask her, otherwise he might explode if he didn't find out. But she didn't have an answer. All she said as she grabbed his arm was ...

"Eh?"

"What?"

"Pardon?"

And she fiddled with her hearing aid, which made a loud screech.

Or at least Stanley thought it was the hearing aid until he realised it was actually a little girl standing near them.

"Look!" the little girl yelled. "Up there. That hotel is on fire!"

Stanley looked up to where she was pointing. Over on the other side of the bay stood a big hotel, right on the edge of the cliff. And a fire was ripping through it.

He had to do something. He had to save the day. But how could he when Nan was holding on to him?

He looked around him for some way of distracting Nan so he could escape and change, but then he saw something odd out at sea. A wave that was getting bigger and bigger. It was the biggest wave he'd ever seen.

It was moving towards the hotel. It was as if someone was blowing the wave that way, but who? Only a superhero could do something like that!!

CHAPTER 7
THE SILVER FLASH!

Stanley watched with his mouth wide open as the wave grew bigger than a skyscraper, and then ... CRASH!! – the wave broke, all over the hotel, putting the fire out in a flash. The building was soggy, but it was safe. And it had to have been saved by the most super of superheroes.

Stanley looked again at Nan. “Please tell me you saw THAT?” he begged.

But Nan just looked out of breath, like she’d run a hundred metres in a world-record time.

"Nan?" Stanley said. "Nan? Are you OK?"

Nan didn't answer. She got redder and redder, and she looked like she was about to explode. Stanley took a step back but didn't know why.

And then Nan sneezed, which blew two cars and a minibus upside down.

"WHOOOOOOOAAAAA!" yelled Stanley. He'd never seen anything like

it. If Nan's sneeze could do that ... then what else did she have the power to do?

"Nan," Stanley said. "That wave ... that was you, wasn't it?"

“I don’t know what you mean,” the old woman said, but she was blushing now.

“Yes you do,” said Stanley as he started to make sense of everything. “And that’s not all you’ve done today. You stopped that plane from crashing, didn’t you?”

Nan said nothing, but Stanley thought he saw her smile.

"And that robber in the bingo hall. It was you that pinned him down with your knitting needles. Don't try and tell me it wasn't!"

Nan's smile just got bigger and bigger and bigger.

"Well, Stanley," she said – getting his name right as if she'd known it all along – "we all have our secrets, don't we? And where do you think you and your dad get your powers from?"

"I ... I ... I always thought it must have been Grandad," said Stanley.

"Grandad? Do me a favour! He was a lovely man, but he couldn't save a penalty, never mind the world! You get your powers from me, because I'm the Silver Flash!"

But just as Stanley was about to hug his nan, a shadow grew above them, so big and dark that it felt like midnight. They both looked up and saw not one, not two, but twelve UFOs waiting to attack.

“Please tell me you have your costume with you?” Nan asked.

“I do,” said Stanley bravely. “But I’m not sure two of us can beat a whole galaxy of aliens.”

“Oh, don’t worry,” Nan said. “I know who we can call for help …

“OLDIES … ASSEMBLE!!!”

There was only ever going to be one side which won that battle. And as Stanley rode home in the coach that night, falling asleep against his nan, he knew they'd had the best day out – ever.

Our books are tested
for children and young people by
children and young people.

Thanks to everyone who consulted on
a manuscript for their time and effort in
helping us to make our books better
for our readers.